Superman: Man of Steel

Senior Editor Matt Jones
Project Art Editor Stefan Georgiou
Production Editor Marc Staples
Senior Production Controller Laura Andrews
Managing Editor Emma Grange
Managing Art Editor Vicky Short
Publisher Paula Regan
Art Director Charlotte Coulais
Managing Director Mark Searle

Reading Consultant Barbara Marinak
Designed for DK by Nicholas Pashourtides

DK would like to thank Victoria Selover and Katie Campbell at Warner Bros. Discovery; Megan Douglass for proofreading and Julia March for proofreading and indexing.

First American Edition, 2025
Published in the United States by DK Publishing, a division of Penguin Random House LLC
1745 Broadway, 20th Floor, New York, NY 10019

Page Design Copyright © 2025 Dorling Kindersley Limited
25 26 27 28 29 10 9 8 7 6 5 4 3 2 1
001–345010–June/2025

Copyright © 2025 DC.
SUPERMAN and all related characters and elements © & ™ DC. WB SHIELD: ™ & © WBEI. (s25)
Superman created by Jerry Siegel and Joe Shuster

All rights reserved.
Without limiting the rights under the copyright reserved above, no part of this publication may be reproduced, stored in or introduced into a retrieval system, or transmitted, in any form, or by any means (electronic, mechanical, photocopying, recording, or otherwise), without the prior written permission of the copyright owner.
Published in Great Britain by Dorling Kindersley Limited

A catalog record for this book
is available from the Library of Congress.
ISBN: 978-0-5939-6576-4 (Paperback)
ISBN: 978-0-5939-6577-1 (Hardcover)

DK books are available at special discounts when purchased
in bulk for sales promotions, premiums, fund-raising,
or educational use.
For details, contact: DK Publishing Special Markets,
1745 Broadway, 20th Floor, New York, NY 10019
SpecialSales@dk.com

Printed and bound in China

www.dk.com

This book was made with Forest Stewardship Council™ certified paper – one small step in DK's commitment to a sustainable future. Learn more at www.dk.com/uk/information/sustainability

Level 3

Superman: Man of Steel

Written by Matt Jones

Contents

6	Meet Superman
8	Superman's origins
10	Martha Kent and Jonathan Kent
12	Growing up
14	Superman's mission
16	Superman's powers
18	Superman's suit
20	Secret identity
22	Krypto
24	*Daily Planet*
26	Lois Lane
28	Jimmy Olsen
30	Perry White
32	Superman's foes
34	Cyborg Superman

36 General Zod
38 Lex Luthor
40 Mister Terrific
42 Supergirl
44 The Justice League
46 Glossary
47 Index
48 Quiz

Meet Superman

Say hello to Superman! Superman is a strong and brave Super Hero. He protects people and fights Super-Villains. Superman is actually an alien from another planet called Krypton. The planet Earth is now Superman's home.

Superman's origins

Superman was born on the planet Krypton. Superman's people are named Kryptonians. Superman's Kryptonian parents, Jor-El and Lara Lor-Van, named him Kal-El. They sent their baby son to Earth in a spaceship to keep him safe.

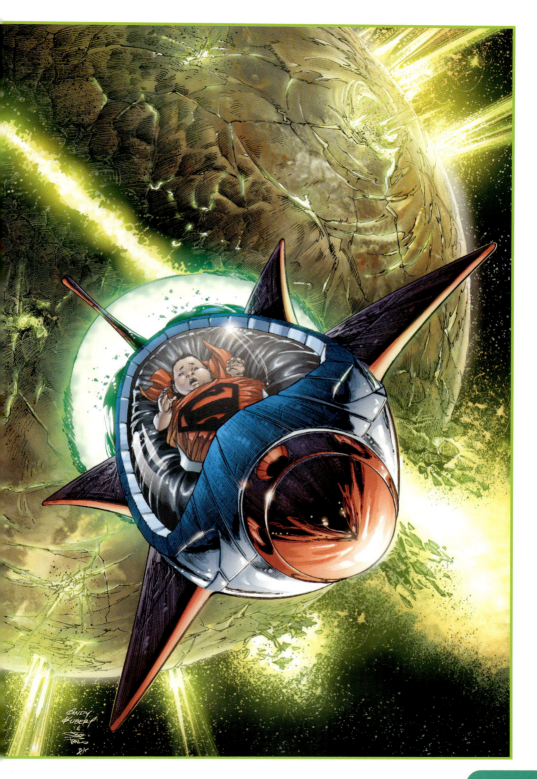

Martha Kent and Jonathan Kent

Martha Kent and Jonathan Kent are farmers. They run a small farm just outside a town named Smallville. One day, they find Kal-El's spaceship in their field. The kind couple decide to adopt Kal-El. They name him Clark Kent.

Growing up

While growing up, Clark discovers that he has amazing superpowers. He goes to school in Smallville and makes friends with Lana Lang. At first, Clark doesn't tell Lana that he has superpowers. However, one day he must use his superpowers to save Lana from a tornado.

Superman's mission

Jonathan and Martha tell Clark to use his superpowers to help people. They don't want Clark to be selfish or mean.
Clark listens to his parents and uses his powers for good when he is older.
Clark becomes a Super Hero!

Superman's powers

Superman has many superpowers because he is a Kryptonian.

Flying
Superman can fly high into the air and can even fly in space.

Heat vision
Superman can release beams of very hot energy from his eyes.

Super-strength
Superman is super-strong. He can lift cars high into the air without getting tired.

X-ray vision
Superman can see through most things to help him understand how they work.

Superman's suit

Superman wears a special suit when he is fighting crime. His suit is blue, red, and yellow. It has an S-shield on it. Superman's suit is made of a special type of cloth. It is very hard to damage Superman's suit.

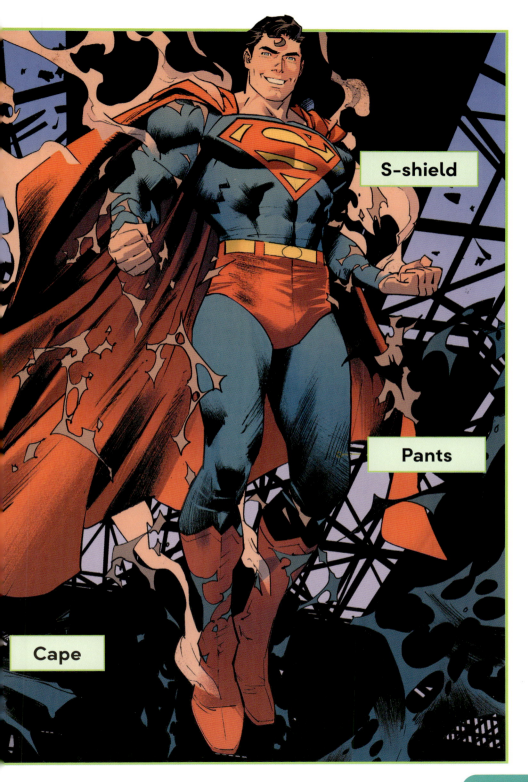

Secret identity

Clark Kent wants to protect his family and friends so he keeps his identity as Superman a secret. No one else can know that Clark Kent is actually a Super Hero. While he is Clark Kent, Superman doesn't wear his special suit but does wear glasses. Nobody notices he is the same person!

Krypto

Krypto is a superpowered dog from the planet Krypton. He is Superman's pet. Krypto is also the leader of the League of Super-Pets. This brave group of powerful pets fights crime.

Daily Planet

When Clark Kent is an adult, he moves to a city named Metropolis. He starts working as a reporter at a newspaper named the *Daily Planet*. Clark becomes good friends with Lois Lane and Jimmy Olsen.

Lois Lane

Lois Lane is a smart newspaper reporter. She has won many awards for her newspaper stories. Lois is brave and is not scared of criminals or Super-Villains. She later marries Clark Kent. They have a son together named Jon.

Jimmy Olsen

Jimmy Olsen is a photographer who works at the *Daily Planet*. He is also best friends with Clark Kent. He figures out that Clark Kent and Superman are the same person. Superman often has to rescue Jimmy from Super-Villains who have captured him.

Perry White

Perry White is an experienced newspaper reporter who is in charge of the *Daily Planet*. He must check all of the stories in the newspaper. Perry is a great teacher, and Clark and Lois have learned a lot from him. Perry is godparent to their son, Jon Kent.

Superman's foes

Superman has many foes who want to try to defeat him. Some of them, like Doomsday, are aliens from other planets. Other villains, like Lex Luthor, are from Earth. Sometimes Superman's foes team up to face him in battle. Will they be able to defeat Superman?

Lex Luthor

Cyborg Superman

Cyborg Superman used to be a human astronaut named Hank Henshaw. One day, his spaceship crashed and he had to transfer his brain into a computer to survive. Even though Superman did nothing wrong, Hank blames Superman for the crash. Hank has built himself a cyborg body. Hank names himself Cyborg Superman. He pretends to be Superman to try to ruin Superman's reputation. Will Superman be able to stop Cyborg Superman?

General Zod

General Zod is a Super-Villain from the planet Krypton. He was a criminal who was captured and kept in a special prison called the Phantom Zone. When Zod escapes his prison, Superman must try to stop him!

Lex Luthor

Lex Luther is a mean scientist and businessperson. He owns a company named LexCorp. Lex used to go to school with Clark Kent. When they are older, Lex learns that Clark is Superman. Lex is jealous of Superman's powers. Lex's employees help him plan ways to defeat Superman.

Mister Terrific

Superman can rely on his ally Mister Terrific. Mister Terrific's real name is Michael Holt, and he is a businessperson. He is very smart and has invented many pieces of technology. Mister Terrific uses his technology to fight Super-Villains. He is also the leader of a Super Hero team named the Terrifics.

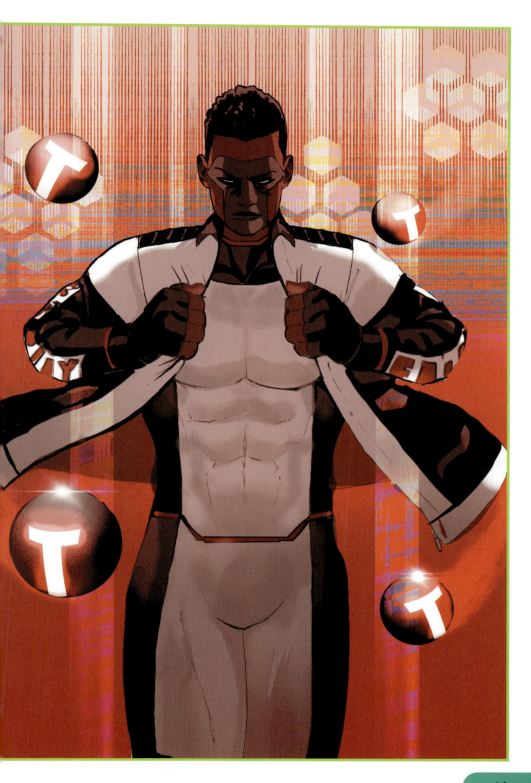

Supergirl

Superman isn't the only Kryptonian Super Hero living on Earth. His cousin Kara Zor-El also crash-landed on Earth. She has the same superpowers as Clark. Kara grew up on Krypton so she is not used to living on Earth. However, she still decides to become a hero like Superman. Now known as Supergirl, Kara is always ready to help her cousin.

The Justice League

The Justice League is a team of powerful Super Heroes. The team works together to defeat the scariest Super-Villains and defend Earth. Superman is a member of the Justice League. His friends Batman, Wonder Woman, Green Lantern, and the Flash are also on the team.

Glossary

alien
someone from a planet other than Earth

crash-land
when a spacecraft lands suddenly and is often damaged

cyborg
someone who is part human, part machine

employee
someone who works for a company or person in exchange for money

godparent
an adult who is chosen by parents to help guide their child as they grow up

inspire
to make you feel excited at the thought of doing something

newspaper reporter
someone whose job is gathering news for a newspaper

reputation
what other people think of someone

superpowers
special powers that most humans don't have

tornado
a dangerous column of rapidly spinning air

x-ray
a beam of radiation that can pass through solid things

Index

Batman 44

Clark Kent 10, 12–13, 14, 20–21, 26, 28, 30, 38, 42

Cyborg Superman 34–35

Daily Planet 24–25, 28, 30

Doomsday 32–33

Flash, the 44

Flying 16

General Zod 36–37

Green Lantern 44

Hank Henshaw 34

Heat vision 16

Jimmy Olsen 24, 28–29

Jon Kent 26, 30

Jonathan Kent 10–11, 14

Jor-El 8

Justice League, the 44–45

Kal-El 8, 10

Kara Zor-El 42–43

Krypto 22–23

Krypton 6, 8, 22, 36, 42

Lana Lang 12–13

Lara Lor-Van 8

League of Super-Pets 22

Lex Luthor 32, 38–39

LexCorp 38

Lois Lane 24, 26–27, 30

Martha Kent 10–11, 14

Metropolis 24

Michael Holt 40

Mister Terrific 40–41

Perry White 30–31

Phantom Zone 36

Smallville 10, 12

super-strength 17

Supergirl 42–43

Superman's suit 18–19

superpowers 16–17

Terrifics, the 40

Wonder Woman 44

X-ray vision 17

Quiz

Are you a Superman expert? Try the quiz to find out!

1. What colors are Superman's suit?
2. Who owns the LexCorp company?
3. Krypto is Superman's pet cat. True or false?
4. Is Jimmy Olsen a photographer?
5. How are Superman and Supergirl related?

1. Red, blue, and yellow 2. Lex Luthor 3. False 4. Yes
5. They are cousins